MADELINE'S CHRISTMAS

MADELINE'S CHRISTMAS

By Ludwig Bemelmans

SCHOLASTIC INC.
New York   Toronto   London   Auckland   Sydney
Mexico City   New Delhi   Hong Kong   Buenos Aires

Sincere thanks to Mrs. Ludwig Bemelmans and Barbara Bemelmans for their help
and advice in adapting and restoring the text and art for *Madelines Christmas,*
and for lending us the few remaining pieces of original art.
For this book, the art has been photographically enlarged and recolored by Jody Wheeler
to prepare it for reproduction.

ISBN 0-439-72175-X

12 11 10 9 8 7 6 5 4 3 2 1   4 5 6 7 8 9/0

Printed in the U.S.A.   08

First Scholastic printing, November 2004

MADELINE'S CHRISTMAS

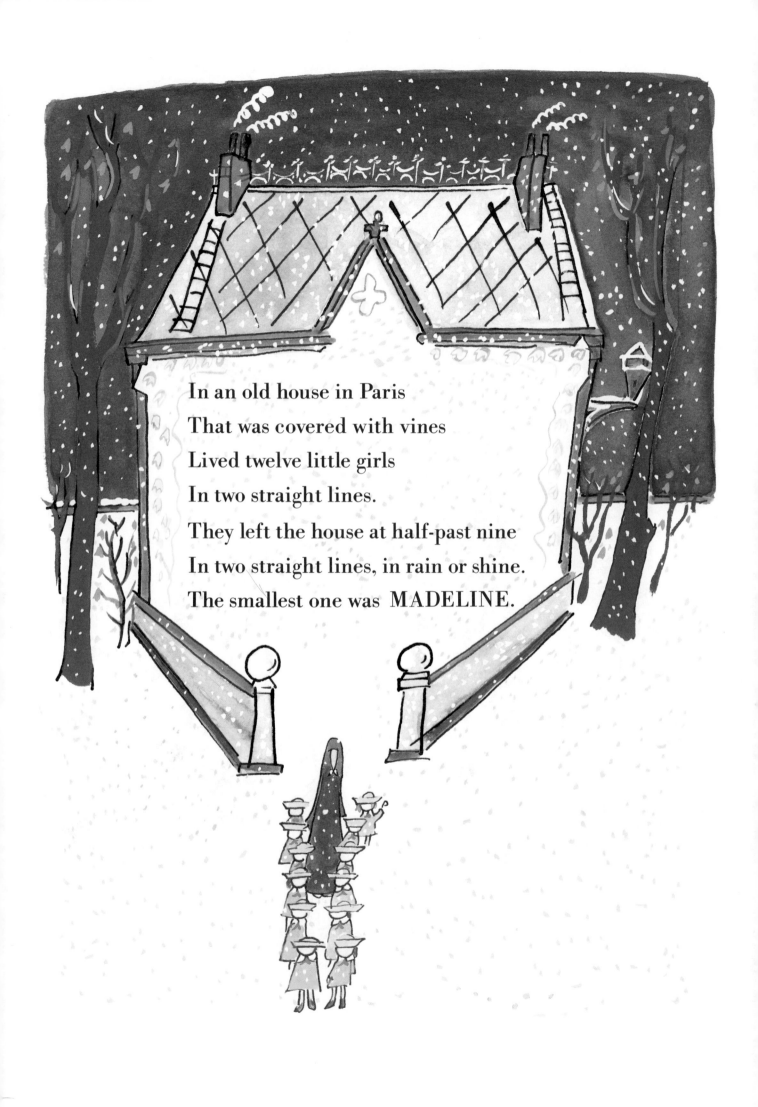

In an old house in Paris

That was covered with vines

Lived twelve little girls

In two straight lines.

They left the house at half-past nine

In two straight lines, in rain or shine.

The smallest one was MADELINE.

She was not afraid of mice

She loved winter, snow and ice

And to the tiger in the zoo

Madeline just said...

"POOH, POOH!"

It was the night before Christmas
And all through the house
Not a creature was stirring
Not even the mouse.

For like everyone else in that house which was old
The poor mouse was in bed with a miserable cold.

And only
Our brave little Madeline

Was up and about

And feeling

Just fine.

Suddenly came a knock
Which made her pause—

Could it perhaps be Santa Claus?
But no…

A rug merchant was at the door.
He had twelve rugs, he had no more.

"Why, these," said Madeline, "would be so neat
For our ice-cold in the morning feet."

"It seems to me," said Miss Clavel,

"That you have chosen very well."

Madeline gave him a handful of francs,
"Here they are with all our thanks."

Without the rugs
Which he had sold
The rug merchant got awfully cold.

"To sell my rugs," he cried, "was silly!
Without them I am very chilly."
He wants to get them back—
But will he?

He made it—back to Madeline's door—
He couldn't take one footstep more.

And little Madeline set about
To find a way to thaw him out.

The merchant, who was tall and thin
(And also a ma-gi-ci-an)
Bravely took his medicine.

The magician, as he took his pill, said
"Ask me, Madeline, what you will."
Said she, "I've cooked a dinner nutritious,
Will you please help me with these dishes?"

"If you'll clear up
I'll go and see
If I can find
A Christmas tree."

His magic ring he gave a glance
And went into a special trance—
The dirty dishes washed themselves
And jumped right back upon the shelves.

And then he mumbled words profound—

"ABRACADABRA"
BRACADABR
RACADAB
ACADA
CAD
A!"

That made the carpets leave the ground—

And twelve little girls were on their way—

To surprise their parents on Christmas Day.